Spectrum

By Kay Kadinger

Jennifer,
Good to meet.
Kim Smith

Music enhancement: Music is a big part of this story. If you'd like to catch the vibe and tone of this story, please consider listening to Stay by 30 Seconds to Mars, Dark Paradise by Lana Del Rey, Fade Into You by Mazzy Star and Human by Christina Perri before or while reading. It's powerful and strange what music can do.

***

Copyright © Kay Kadinger 2015

No reproduction without permission
All rights reserved.

The right of Kay Kadinger to be identified as the author of this work has been asserted by her in accordance with sections 77 and 78 of the Copyright, Designs and Patents Act 1988.

This book is a work of fiction. Names, characters and incidents are either a product of the author's imagination or are used fictitiously. Any resemblance to actual people, living or dead or events is entirely coincidental.

PART ONE

The Beginning

Sam

It started out innocently enough. We have all had the conversations, but ours took a wrong turn. So *many* wrong turns in our Great Perhaps.

Remember when you promised me the Great Perhaps? I think that was when I fell in love with you. I'm certain that if you had ever described it to anyone else in your whole life, you wouldn't have been there looking for me. That empty space beside you would have been filled long ago.

"You're my—" you said. When you spoke, the cadence of your voice had two colors. It was strange because the two colors couldn't have been more different. You have this way of talking. As your words build and you become confident of yourself, blue pops and makes itself known, but when you falter and let the words linger in the air, there's a milky haze and I'm inclined to think white rules your world.

"My what?" I started to smile in a flirty grin, but something about you froze that fake part of me and all you got was me, stripped of all the socially-acceptable gestures and replaced with just me. Goofy, awkward me, and I flashed you a toothy grin instead. I can't even say I meant to, but every part of me wanted you, even my smile. It warmed my insides and crept up all the way to my throat.

"My new Great Perhaps, of course," you said.

"Of course. How could I not know? But tell me again." I walked over to the condiment counter in Little Mae's Forever Flav's and dumped another sugar in my coffee. I needed some space and time to read your color. You weren't backing down, and showed no signs of slowing. How was I supposed to keep myself together?

There was a boy feeding a machine that turns pennies into souvenirs. As the handle turned, rusty waves of orange and brown swirled around the coffee shop, and I got caught up in the cogs and wheels surely turning inside.

"Sam—can I call you Sam? I have to tell you, I find it amusing when beautiful girls have boy names," you said.

You were on your feet and standing behind me, toying with me. Your breath was at the back of my neck as you explained in a blue whisper and looked coyly around the coffee shop, adding tension to an already maple-thick, tension-filled room.

"You ever meet someone, Sam, and you just know? Well, maybe you don't know for sure if she's the one, but something inside says that she's the Great Perhaps. The one that you've been looking for when you didn't even know you were looking. The one you see yourself swimming in oceans with, the one you see yourself making breakfast in bed for, and the one you actually want to stick around?"

Spectrum

My breath caught and I almost laughed as I gave myself instructions to breathe. I remember thinking, *What the hell is going on here?* I didn't know, but I didn't want it to stop. I knew it would, though, once you found out.

I had a dozen thoughts running through my head. *I don't have time for this. I'm already in love with someone else and there's no room for a third party in our love affair.* All thirty-six inches and twenty-four pounds of piss and vinegar with a dash of that sugar and spice would be the only thing to shape my path for at least the next fifteen years.

In another lifetime maybe we would have had some sort of shot, but even then it didn't make sense. It had to be some kind of joke. You're gorgeous in this earthy, lumberjack kind of way. The kind of guy who probably used to be some hotshot football player, but has now outgrown his childish good looks and grown into a man. The kind of man who doesn't need a line like *The Great Perhaps*.

Even before you approached me, I knew who you were. You were in my freshman speech class; a meathead jock type except for you always had a book within your fingertips. I had a distant crush on you. The kind you have on Wolverine when you're more into the cool factor than any of the abs that hide beneath it. You were quiet and shy back then, and colored red through and through— nothing like you are now. You dropped out before the semester was over, but I never stopped thinking about you. There was blue in there somewhere. You just hadn't found it yet. Blue is actually halfway rare, that's why I remembered you.

"Are you still here with me, Sam?" You leaned in to whisper, and everything inside me churned.

I turned around and put my hands up, then gently pushed you out of the way. But then you grabbed me by the arm. If it had been anyone else, it might have been alarming; instead it only magnified what I was already feeling. Which in simple terms was anything but rational. I wanted you to take me from the coffee shop right then and there. I didn't even care if we made it to the car. I wanted you so bad it hurt.

"How about it then?"

"What?" My voice croaked as I fought hard not to be embarrassed. I'd just made it obvious the effect you had on me.

"The Great Perhaps. Whahadya say?"

Right then I decided. *It's time to end this now before it gets out of hand.* I'd already let myself go past the next ten minutes and onto breakfast in bed, knowing the heartache of wanting to keep you would be worse than any pleasure I could have gotten right then and there. My head had started to clear and I remember being thankful for it and grieving at the same time. *Always the good girl.*

"I have a kid." I looked you square in the eyes and waited.

You laughed and then settled into a smile. "I know. So do I."

Chapter One

Sam

Indigo Blue and all its Hues

"What do you mean you hear colors?" Ben asks and takes a bite of my cheese ravioli, even though this is only our second official date.

I push the plate to his side, as I'm beginning to lose my appetite. His voice is innocently enough yellow, but maybe I'm reading him wrong.

"Feel them too. It's not that big of a deal. I'm sure lots of people do."

He smirks a bit followed by some kind of half-hearted laugh, yellow vibrating so loud it's as if the sun has exploded in the tiny Italian restaurant.

"Come on, you're pulling my leg."

I don't really talk about it, although I've known for years. I smile a little to myself as I consider Ben to be an old soul.

"Ben, this is for your own good. I need to tell you something."

Yellow. Yellow. Yellow.

He's waiting expectantly.

"No one born after 1939 says *pulling my leg*."

"Come on, don't divert." A new intensity is turning him blue. "What do you mean you hear and feel colors?" His arms are folded and he's waiting for me to say more, his own food long gone. A plate clatters to the floor behind him and he jumps slightly.

"That was black." I'm testing him.

"Broken dishes are black?" Apprehension skitters across his face.

"Anything loud, chaotic. Anything that doesn't belong."

"Get out." He chuckles.

"It's real, it's called synesthesia."

His hand instinctively reaches for his phone.

I feel my left eyebrow rise in challenge. "Google?"

"Do you have superpowers?" He reaches for my hand instead.

"It benefits no one but me."

"How so?"

"Do you like art? Music?"

"Who doesn't?" He smiles as he leans in closer. Now *he* pushes the ravioli aside.

"I see it differently."

"How so?"

"That information is strictly for third dates."

"Clever girl. I knew there was a Great Perhaps here."

A few weeks later...

"I don't know. He doesn't know you and it feels weird. I always told myself I wasn't going to be one of those girls who brings a new guy around her kid every other week."

I drop my backpack down and stare into the fireplace.

Spectrum

It burns with steady confidence. Fire never shows weakness. Give it a spark, and it will eat you alive.

"Come on, Sam. Work with me here," Ben says with a wink as he steps in front of the fire, his own flames dancing just below the surface. He crouches down and into my space.

"You wink too much. It makes you seem too smooth." I back up just out of his reach.

In my weirdness with new relationships, we're trying friendship first, but I'm not sure how much longer I can hold him off.

"Winking is a sign of trust. Try to wink angrily at me. Go ahead. It's impossible."

I find myself actually doing it, when suddenly he leans in closer and his lips brush close to mine.

I freeze.

"God, you're gorgeous," he says as he draws closer, until his mouth is at my ear.

I'm not going to be able to avoid the blue much longer.

"It's been two months. This protective mom thing is pretty sexy, but you trust me by now, don't you? I swear I never have, nor will I *ever* own a big white van." He smiles and slouches back into his chair. He has the back of his head resting between laced fingers, and I'm now certain of his ex-jock status. He clears his throat. "Besides, what choice do you have?"

I rush home from my art class and don't find the apartment in shambles. I don't find the kitchen on fire. I don't find Tate in tears, missing Mommy or screaming for me to come home. They're playing. A strange game with plastic figurines and nothing else. They are in the same world and talking about something I'm sure I'll never understand. I swallow hard. This is unusual for Tate. He's animated and concentrating more than I've ever seen him. Tate's a quiet boy who plays noiselessly with these figures, usually in a corner somewhere. Silently asking not to be bothered.

"How did you do that?" I ask, a little shaken.

"What?" Ben's lying on the floor, his weight distributed to one elbow as he glances back up to me.

I plop down on the floor, but the game has stopped. Tate scoops up his toys and puts them back in the old Star Wars lunch box, leaving a few behind for Ben. The latch closes with an orange squeak.

"Hey Buddy, you need to find your clone troopers. We have a battle to fight. Next time, okay?"

Tate sees me watching Ben and looks at me in yellow, inquisitive. It seems as if Tate wants to ask me something, but he scampers off instead. I look back to Ben.

"You know I never even saw these until I was a freshman in high school." He says as he turns Darth Vader over in his hands.

"Toys?" I give him a wary smile.

"These kind. My parents were never really around. Spent most of my time with the TV. I've seen all the movies I guess, but this is so much better." He pretends to walk his guy over to me. "Tate's lucky to have a mom like you."

Spectrum

"What gives?" I ask Ben as he sits up and we sit facing each other cross-legged, knees barely touching, and I wonder why people don't sit on the floor more often. The perspective feels more honest somehow.

"Sorry?" he asks.

"What are you in this for?" I feel anger boil up out of nowhere. The moment before, the sweetness of Tate's happiness long gone, and now I just want to know. "Listen, I don't know what you're up to, but this isn't some kind of game. You can't go and make my kid love you without talking to me about it first."

"I wasn't expecting that," he says. He looks down and fiddles with a few strands of carpet.

"What's your story? You didn't tell me you were good with kids."

"I'm not. I mean, I'm usually not. There's something about him. Something that reminds me of me. God, Sam. He's great."

He keeps talking, but my insides feel like liquid and I'm finding it hard to concentrate.

This is supposed to be Jude talking. Ben is taking it from him and I'm not ready. Tate's not ready. A vision of what Jude might have looked like three years after he died flashes through my head and, as great as Ben is, it's infuriating. I don't want this. I only want Jude. Maybe in someone else's Great Perhaps, but this is laced with betrayal. It might have worked if I had come in the door and Ben was watching TV, playing with his phone, or eating my leftovers out of the fridge. I wasn't expecting this. To come in and see the two of them the way they were. It was a mistake.

"Whoa, something's changed," Ben says, and I look up to him, not realizing I had scooted away.

"This is wrong, Ben. I can't explain it, but you've overstepped."

"It's not wrong. I can't explain it either, but I know it's not wrong. What color would you call it? What's the color for it when it's right?"

"Indigo."

"This is indigo."

"Why?"

He stands up and paces around a little. I want to kick him out and give myself time to think.

"Listen, I had a family once. They've been gone a while, but it's still not easy. And I've just gotten to a point where I'm okay with it. Life happens, right? God, that sounds harsh, but you know what I mean. They're gone, and there's nothing I can do about it."

He has a white cloud of unease around him, but I can't help myself. "What happened?"

He starts to shift as he sits on the floor, and the black is mixing with the white. Something's off, dark and twisted. He's working over something in his mind and rust is starting to peak out, but I can feel the color dissipate as he covers it with orange, rebellious. He's fighting something.

"Tate sort of brought it all back. Something was missing. I want that. I have Brooke, but her mother controls all of that. I didn't know how bad I wanted a family."

"Get out."

"What'd I say? Shit, I didn't mean it like that. I don't

Spectrum

mean I want to be his father. I just want to be there for him. He needs it too."

I glance at Tate's room and the door is closed. "How the hell would you know what he needs? Get out!"

He doesn't fight me. The front door closes and he's gone before I can change my mind.

"I'm sorry, Jude," I say to myself.

I feel myself sliding down the inside of the door until finally my body collapses to the ground, knees up, and I start crying into the crook of my elbow. It's for the best. Better to know now. Better than down the road when he's done me wrong, cheated on me, gotten bored and moved on, or worse. There's always worse. The irreversible worse.

I can't get myself to leave the spot I've heaped myself in. The mother in me demands I get up and see what duties I should perform for Tate. Duties to bring me back to the only place I feel comfortable. I'd have never survived the loss of Jude if it hadn't been for Tate. He was the medicine to pull me out, and I'd been getting daily doses since before he was even born.

But the door feels blue. Or something sitting outside that door.

I stand and open it. In his lean Ben falls back a little, only a door separating us. It startles me a little when I realize we'd being sitting like mimes on opposite sides of a mirror.

"I can fix this," he says in a voice hoarse from emotion backed up and unused.

I let the door swing open, and he walks in assuredly. He removes my hand from the knob and hooks one of my fingers in his belt loop, then shuts the door and turns the deadbolt. My finger is stilled looped, tied to him. I don't want any of him. I want all of him.

Together we walk to the back bedroom, and the anxiety of Tate being doors away flutters red in my chest as we sweep past his bedroom. I peek through the crack of Tate's door. He's curled in a ball, Toy Story playing in the background, and his chest heaves in a deep contentment of slumber only children can achieve. I smile nervously as Woody tries to convince Buzz he's a toy.

Ben shuts my bedroom door. He's never been in here before, and I watch him appraise the room, taking in each item, cataloging it in his mind somewhere, quickly studying everything but the bed. He walks over to the old stereo I have on the dresser and scans the CDs I have strewn about. He puts in River Rats, walks into the bathroom that attaches to the bedroom, and turns the shower on.

I sit on the bed and watch him, half expecting Tate to wake and knock softly on the door. Half of me wants that, and the other half... well, I'm not sure.

He walks back out and unwraps the heap of hair that was resting in a messy bun toward the base of my neck. He lingers on the ends, flipping it through his fingers. My stomach is wound tight and, if I admit it to myself, I'm nervous he'll see how inexperienced I am. There's been only Jude, but if I'm going to pull this off I can't think of him now.

He leads me to the shower and my hands are trembling. I've wanted him before. Desperately. But that's not what this is. I'm terrified.

"Now's your chance to back out. We can wait. I will wait for you, always. If you need more time, tell me now."

I say nothing.

He removes my t-shirt first, and it feels like he is drinking me in. The rest of the clothes come off in a blur, and I blush as he catches me taking all of him in. Is this really happening?

He stands behind me in a shower built for two, but only ever used by one, and moves my wet hair that hangs like ropes. Then he begins to scrub my back, softly scratching with only his fingernails, and I let my head hang to stretch the tension out of my neck. He kisses my shoulder blades and my body explodes in a new color. I could have a thousand words to describe the spectrum and it still wouldn't be enough. It's like a sunset that's been destroyed by a nuclear bomb. It's the red of all things unknown—screaming at me that I'll *never* know—the orange of blind rebellion, and the black ash of something not right, but with no power to deny. But there's also that blue.

I turn to him before I have time to change my mind, and let him take me. Take me somewhere I've never been. A place where rules don't matter, time is just an idea, and loss is something we get to forget.

Chapter Two

Sam

Two Years Later

When I first started thinking about Ben and the Great Perhaps, I never considered that Tate would fit into Ben's version. In some ways, Tate fits better than even I do. Watching the two of them stabs with the pain of what Jude will never be, followed by the soft Band-Aid of what Ben is.

"When are you going to make an honest man out of me?" Ben smiles from bed as I bump the door open with my behind to further accommodate the tray.

"Mommy!" Tate scrambles in behind me and I almost dump the plates.

I only smile at him because we've had the conversation a few times now. He knows I'll say yes, but he's waiting for confirmation, testing the waters again.

"Come here, little dude. Mom's got pancakes and bacon, I can smell it." Ben growls. "Pancakes for me and bacon for you!" He pokes Tate in the chest and I die a little inside. How could I possibly say no?

Tate (all five years of him) flops onto Ben's chest and through muffled boy cries I hear "pancakes, pancakes, pancakes!" He flips his head back to me as if to check, and I nod.

I set the tray down. Ben scoops the bacon off and devours it in one bite.

"You're next," he says as if reading my thoughts, and I sit beside him on the creaky bed.

"Tate has to go to his grandparents this weekend." I wipe the bacon grease off the side of his mouth and he swipes his tongue at me.

"How long have I been doing this with you, Sam?" He flips Tate to the other side of the bed, then Frisbee flies a pancake at him and it flops on his lap. Tate's eyes widen, but then he digs in and we are long forgotten, forsaken for Bisquick.

"I have a surprise for you." He grins mischievously, but I shouldn't really describe it that way anymore. That's just the way Ben smiles.

"When will you get Brooke? Because I've been doing this with you too, and it always changes."

Ben's ex-wife is about as flaky as Tate's pancakes, and that's not me being the bitter girlfriend, that's just the way it is.

"Her mom said not this weekend, so we have the weekend all to ourselves."

He flips the covers off and exits the bed in just a pair of silk lounge pants. Even if I see this every day for the rest of my life, I will still take the time to watch him get out of bed. He's never more beautiful than at this particular part of the day. His dark blond hair flops in his face and he rubs at his five o'clock shadow as he lumbers toward the bathroom. He's thirty, but still looks eighteen. Every part of him is chiseled in a gentle reminder of my current lucky streak. I keep waiting for the joke to be over. I'll never deserve him. I've wondered before if he has body dysmorphic disorder, and either doesn't know how beautiful he is or how beautiful I'm not. I've never said anything to him, because I'm afraid if I say it out loud he'll realize it too. Plus, I'd rather not be that insecure girl who needs her man to tell her how great she is. Needy, wanting, begging for affirmation. I'm all those things, but I'll never let him know.

I hear the shower turn on and realize as the spigot rains down on him that I have my own storm brewing. I don't even hear him walk back out from his notorious thirty-second showers. He's wearing only a white towel against his beautifully tan skin.

"What's wrong?" Gone is his flashy grin as he wipes my tears away. "I'll be right back."

I hear him scoop Tate up and promise him cartoons, and barely hear the door shut and lock as he comes back in.

"Talk or fix?" he asks as he tightens up the towel at his waist and leans back down to kiss away another tear.

"Fix."

He understands and walks over to the CD player, puts in River Rats, and turns it up loud enough to muffle anything that shouldn't be heard by a five-year-old. Then he walks back over, looks at me, and waits for direction. The CD lands on a song where Hugo Wiley sings perfectly pink and I can feel the heat blush my cheeks, wondering if Ben really knows me that well or if he's just gotten lucky.

"Chair," I say.

He picks me up smoothly and I wrap my legs around him, then he sets me into his lap in our big overstuffed chair, put in the room for this very reason.

As I ease down on him I feel that he's ready, and I brace myself to get lost in Ben. He'll take me away from this. I take his mouth in mine, hungry as my hips instinctively reach for him. His hands are behind my neck—softly now, but soon they will be hungry and there will always be too much space between us.

"I want it the way it used to be," he says. "It's like we don't talk anymore. I want what's in here." He taps on my chest. Orange radiates from me, rebellious. He'll not have all of me yet. Not when this is so good.

I put my finger to his mouth. "Shhhhh, please take me."

He nods.

He unleashes his towel and every part of me wants him. Blue flashes in a pink and white room, as if lightening breaks free from a rose colored cloud. He lifts my arms into the air and they stay suspended as he slips his t-shirt off me and slides his fingers down my arms, then the bare skin beside my breasts, and down to my newest Victoria Secret purchase before he rips the lacy underwear off, not wanting to part even for the short amount of time it would take to remove them. My arms fall back down and I pull at the back of his hair. I bring his mouth down to my breasts and I arch my back. This will be his breaking point and he will take me, but not before teasing me just because he can.

He moves his hand down and finds my sweet spot.

Then his fingers creep further inside me and he teases until he takes me to a place I've never known with anyone else. A place he now belongs. He pauses and looks at me with a wanting, almost sad smile before he starts stroking his fingers back and forth, and I'm sick from how bad I need him. I can have him if I choose, but I know he wants it slow. I let him continue, but move so his hand is removed and I'm rubbing on top of him. His nails claw at my back and I rock. I need him inside, but give it just a few more seconds. Then I lean in and nibble at his ears, and he breaks.

He shoves himself into me and I almost get there just from the very first push. He scoots down a bit and the control is mine. I rock until I can't keep it in any longer, then I let go. As all the nerve endings fire and a warmth rushes to my lower back, I push one last time, going as deep as my body will allow, and he sets himself free to be with me.

Chapter Three

Sam

Two years ago – Four Days after the coffee shop

Twilight teases at the skyline as the church looms in the background, a single cross pirouetting as it shakes and rattles in the wind. I should be going. These gravel roads that will lead me out of the cemetery become vague at best when the sun disappears.

I stand up, brush the dirt from my jeans, and look around. I consider that it's probably weird I lie over the spot where he rests. I know he's not in there, but this is all I have left. Lots of lost souls here. Some taken too soon, but maybe it's always too soon when it's someone you love. I scan quickly past the small headstone that bears the name of a child. I've never liked that one. Another reminder that fate doesn't care how old you are or the plans you have for your life. I look down at the one who keeps bringing me out here.

Jude Van Erem
December 21, 1988-January 2011
Beloved Son

It should say beloved father, but we never got that far.

Walking back to the car, the gravel crunches beneath my tennis shoes and I'm so wrapped up in my own grief that I barely see him standing there. My heart lurches and, instead of the fear I should feel, I realize it's embarrassment. He's seen me. Watched me get up from lying on a lonely grave. There's no one actually there, just the remains of a life taken too soon and the imprint of a girl who can't let go.

"Don't be alarmed," he says with hands in surrender. He looks embarrassed and curious at the same time, the yellow a match for the sun that crests behind him as he leans against my car.

"What are you doing here, Ben?"

"I followed you."

"That's not creepy."

"I know. And I almost didn't come in. I parked up by the entrance and then just found myself walking around. I knew you were in here somewhere and I couldn't help myself."

The last of the sun disappears and I try to open the sticky latch of my Honda Accord. He's watching me struggle to put away the candle I've had burning, which is still warm with false comfort, and the radio I use to play the songs that tie me to the boy who lies in the ground. A tear slips and drops to my shaky hand as the candle wobbles and the latch continues to stick. The candle drops and hot wax spills onto my foot, seeping into the thin mesh of my running shoe.

Ben fumbles the radio out of my hand and hastily sets it on the ground, then begins to untie my shoe slowly and removes my sock. It sticks a little as the wax is already drying, and he skims the pink skin of my tender foot.

"What are you doing here?" I ask again as I pull my foot back. I hop around a little and finally get the latch open.

"I needed to see you again."

"You couldn't find a way to do it that was a little less Fatal Attraction?"

"I know, I'm sorry. My methods aren't always great, but my intentions are. What are *you* doing out here? I couldn't help but notice, Van Erem. I remember that name. Terrible car accident, wasn't it?" He shifts a little as he stares toward Jude's grave.

He says it nervously. He must be one of those people who are uncomfortable in cemeteries. I can't say I blame him. It's probably the most appropriate way to feel. Sometimes I forget about what a freak I am. This place is home to me and the only place I can still feel Jude.

Tears are slipping out again. I don't even know this guy and he's making me feel things I'm trying to put away. It's like the creamed corn in the pantry. You always have some on hand, and someday you might need to use it, but it's better off toward the back where you can forget about it. Food drive comes around once in a while and you pull it out from deep within the cupboard. A chance to clean house and make room for things you actually can use. But you don't let it go, just shove it back further. Taking up space when you don't have any.

"Do you want to talk about it?" He looks sincere and the blue is there more than ever, but I'm not sure why. He doesn't belong here, but maybe neither do I.

"This is none of your business." I clear my throat to stifle the emotion. Emotion he's not entitled to.

"It might help. Having someone to listen. You could

tell me about him."

I can still hear him talking, something about grief and all the stages, but all I can think about is Jude. Thoughts of him *turning in his grave* have my face flushing hot.

"I can help you. Let me help you fix this," he says as he lets his hand hover above my heart, careful not to touch me yet.

There's about a million reasons why what he just said was dysfunctional, but he's so blue. Blue, that impossible color, that's blue only for me.

Chapter Four

Sam

The List – Now

"Moving in? That's a big step." I've just loaded the last box into the U-Haul truck and, even with all of our stuff combined, it's only half full. "Are you really, really sure?"

"I want to move past the Great Perhaps, doll. You're the one I want." He comes behind me for a hug as we look outside the truck. I say goodbye to apartment living with just me and Tate, and hello to a rental house with Ben, and part-time living with his daughter Brooke, who at best stays with us once a month.

"This is serious, Ben." I turn around so I can read his face. I'm waiting to catch him in some lie that doesn't take his mouth to tell.

"I am serious. This is what I want."

"You're not nervous? One person for the rest of your life? What about all the other missed chances? What if there's a better fit for you out there somewhere?"

"Jeeze, we're just moving in. It's not like we're getting married or anything." He scowls at me as he jumps off the back of the truck and gives me his hand to help me down.

I refuse. "Really?" I scowl back. There's a bit of brat in me today.

"What'd I do? What more do you want from me? We're living together. I think that's a pretty big deal."

"I can't do this. If this isn't forever for you, we can't do it. I have Tate to think about. I'd like to avoid the revolving door of boyfriends."

"I'd like that too," he says, but it doesn't come out sweet. It's cloaked with snarky. He paces around before he says, "That's not what I meant." He exhales deeply and considers what to say next.

"You're the one. What more can I say? All I want is you."

"How can you be so sure?" It sickens me that I'm being *that* girl. "Okay," I say as I hop off the truck. I want to lighten the mood and I have to think fast.

I take him by the hand and sit him down on the cement steps that lead to a life I'm ready to leave behind. "If we do this, I don't want you stuck with me. At any point, you can tell me if it's not working. Don't feel bad for me. I can handle whatever it is, as long as it's real."

"I'm not going anywhere." He puts his arm around me and brings me in close. His crisp, Irish Spring scent makes me want to own him.

"Okay, now. Let's make it official. Let's do the *Friends* thing," I say with a little laugh and turn toward him.

"Am I supposed to know what you're talking about?"

"I don't want to keep you from anything. Pick the famous person you'd like to sleep with if there were no consequences to our relationship. Your List."

Understanding registers. "Free pass? People don't

really do that." He smiles.

"Sure they do. Yes," I say as I think about it a little more, and I can feel the impish smile taunting him. "Just like Ross and Rachel. Remember his was Isabella Rossellina?"

"Yeah, I remember." He laughs. "That was some funny shit. *It's laminated.* I remember."

"So pick." I poke him softly in the side.

"Samantha Witherspoon," he says as he stands and gets down on one knee. "This isn't happening right now, but I can tell you, for the rest of my life, I will want no one but you." He kisses my hand and leans in to plant one on my mouth.

"Okay then, it's just for fun. Give me a name." I don't know what I'm doing. Maybe somewhere deep inside I want to know who he feels is his ideal and compare myself to her. Maybe if I'm close, this could work. If she has dark hair, blue eyes, and a build that was once athletic but now ordinary, maybe this could work for me and Ben.

"Jennifer Lopez." Damn. That was probably the worst possible answer.

But instead I smile. "Yes, there's your list. Would you like an alternate?"

"Can you be my alternate?" He pokes me back.

"So you want permission to cheat on me with me?" I stifle a giggle.

"Is that an option? If it is, I'm changing my answer."

"No, no, we'll stick with JLo. What is it? Her ass?"

"She has nice skin." He smiles sheepishly. "Let's even this up, darlin'. Give me *your* answer." He picks me up and pins me to the side of the building, and I almost get lost in the smolder of this thing called Ben.

I nip at his neck. "That's easy. Lead singer for the River Rats."

"So if I lose you, it's going to be to a guy who probably screws a dozen girls a week and has the payment plan for treating STDs down at the local clinic." He takes a handful of my hair and inhales, noticing the shampoo that smells like apples I use just for him.

"Hey." I bite at his ear. "This was just for fun. It's not like it's ever going to happen. If I ever met him, I'd still choose you. I'll cheat on you with you."

"Alright, alright." He traces my lower lip with his thumb. "But I would feel a little better if your celebrity crush was Larry King or something."

Chapter Five

Sam

"So what's this big surprise?" I turn to Ben, who's tapping his fingers nervously on the steering wheel, and we watch the last of Tate go through his grandparents' doorway, the shimmer of a Teenage Mutant Ninja Turtles backpack disappearing into the arms of his grandmother.

"Well, you're not getting that, but I will tell you it's happening now, and it's very top secret. Your bags are packed and in the back."

"You're awfully yellow," I say.

He doesn't even bother to hide his colors now. What would be the point?

"Curious?" He grins. "You should be the one who's curious. I'm the man with the surprise." He glances back toward Tate's grandparents as we pull away. "What are they like?"

"I've told you before, Tate's fine."

Ben might as well be Tate's dad. He's the guy who hovers when Tate's mastering a new skill. The guy who interferes at conferences and asks if he's getting enough one on one attention. The guy who asks too many questions about his grandparents.

"I know. Just yellow, I guess."

"You can meet them if you want."

"I'm good," he says, "that wouldn't be awkward or

anything."

We drive for two hours. He doesn't think I've noticed, but I've seen signs with arrows pointing that say "Wedding this way!" leading all the way up to what looks like an old colonial bed and breakfast with sprawling grounds. There are other lodges and cottages, but he pulls into the main area where guests are unloading their cars. My hand is trembling so I steady it on the dash. The conspirator glance Ben gave Tate when we dropped him off flashes in my mind, along with the fact that I got the voicemail of all the friends I tried to call on the way. Not a single one answered. What is he up to?

He puts the car into park and turns toward me, watching me expectantly.

"Is this really happening?"

"Yes, surprise! You always tell me I need to be more romantic. What could be more romantic than a weekend getaway at a Bed and Breakfast? Just you and me. An adventure."

"What are we going to do all weekend? Who else is here?" I look at him skeptically, and hurt flashes across his face.

"This is for just you and me, babe. Listen, I know things have been off, but this could get us back."

I never said anything was off, but apparently he can feel it too. I'm surprised he wants to fix whatever it is that's wrong with me. He gets more sex now than he ever has, and I don't even make him work for it. We have a deal. He asks if we should talk or he can "fix it." I never say talk. I think any man would take that deal.

Why is he pushing this?

He is at my side of the car opening the door before I can think about it anymore.

"Come on, let's go check in." He takes my hand and we walk up to the entry, then I see the sign.

BEAVER/KUNTZ WEDDING

"That's a joke, right?" I laugh, and he sees it and starts laughing too. Guests checking in are starting to notice us, and we sneak in before they run us off. I'm starting to feel more and more like the punch line.

When we check in, I see it's one of Ben's friends working the counter.

"Sandy!" He holds his arms out as if to say *I'm here*, and she beams as practically skips over to give him a hug.

"You remember Sam." He gestures to me, but all I can see is her hand lingering on the tail of his shirt. He nonchalantly brushes it away and steps toward me.

Her long blonde hair sways as she is practically vibrating from excitement. "This is going to be such a fun weekend for you guys. I so wish I wasn't working, but I'll be here anyway."

"What's going on?" I ask.

"There's a wedding. You guys are lucky I got you that cottage. Last minute cancellation, and the wait list is a mile long, but I'd do anything for Ben here. It's not just a regular wedding either. Some big wig from The Cities has a daughter getting married, and he pulled out all the stops."

Part of me is relieved. Part of me disappointed. So the wedding's not mine. Such a fool to think we were at that place. I'm not fool enough to think we can last this way much longer. Blissful on the surface. Empty inside. Beautiful blue until we start unwrapping the white layers. He's hiding something, and so am I.

Sandy clears her throat and leans in closer. "If anyone asks, you tell them that you had this planned a year ago and it's your anniversary weekend. Big Daddy wanted the whole place to himself for the wedding party and guests, but I got you in because Ben said you were a fan."

"A fan of what? Weddings?" I look at her like she has lost her head. They must think I'm a complete idiot.

"River Rats. God, Ben, you haven't told her anything, have you?" Then she actually has the decency to look embarrassed. "Not just River Rats either. King's Frat and Blue Baby will be here too. Flown in special just for the wedding."

"Sandy, I really appreciate this. Seriously, you're the best. But if it's all the same, maybe we can catch up later, after we get settled into our room?"

"Yes, of course, it's going to get busy here. Best to get you settled in now, and if you can, lay low. The big wig's a total control freak. Even if you had a reservation, if he finds out you're not part of the wedding party, he might try to get you *removed*," she says with air quotes.

"You let me worry about that." He drapes his arm around my shoulder protectively and swipes the key. "I'll square up when we leave, cool?"

"This one's on me." She winks.

"No, you can't do that. I want to take care of it."

"Trust me, it's easier this way. But you owe me one.

Spectrum

Now get out of here." She shoos us away and we are out the door. I'm stunned.

Everything is abuzz. When I look around, I'm trying not to stare like a complete moron. There are famous people everywhere. Famous for The Cities anyway. It's like a private festival of bands. I see Blue Baby first. She looks even more striking in person. Her long jet black hair hangs low and is streaked with electric blue. She looks up from her entourage, but looks right passed me and onto Ben before giving an approving nod, and then dismisses us.

When I look out around the grounds, I see ginormous white tents everywhere. I sneak a peek at Ben, and he's just as starstruck as I am.

Ben's smiling like a fat cat who just swallowed a mouse as he strolls toward the car in a hurried manner. He nervously checks the key again, and scans for the cabin that will be ours for the weekend. There's something dangerous going on here. Is it because we are not supposed to be here and are essentially wedding crashers? Or maybe it's because we're leaving behind our normal lives where we behave like old parents, a marriage gone stale before it even started.

As the hum of the engine purrs, I look over at my beautiful boyfriend and promise myself to enjoy him for the next couple of days. There's a feeling I can't shake that something's going to change this weekend. I want him this way forever. Young, carefree, full of life. Sweet, engaging, tempting. But he's also gone. He's somewhere exotic. The fairies are dancing behind his sparkling eyes, but I'm not there with him. Somewhere inside my head they are dancing too, but he's not with me.

The cabin appears and it's like a scene from Hansel and Gretel. The siding could be made from candy, the roof of marshmallows. In fact, the name of the cabin is 'Fairytales.'

He unpacks the bags. The sexual tension between us is off the charts, and there's a tight ball wound within the confines of my jeans waiting to explode. Something needs fixing. I move slowly, careful always to keep my eyes on him—waiting, watching, wondering. When will he take me? I breathe in the lilac and take in the bands warming up in the background. A warm summer breeze chills me as I walk through the front door. The floorboards invite me in with a creak, welcome.

Ben is frantically opening all the windows and shades, and has tossed our bags carelessly on the floor. I practically trip over one as I stumble around the bare room that contains only a bed and a mini fridge. There's a white door that must lead to the bathroom, but really that's all there is here.

I open the fridge and it's lined with teeny, tiny liquor bottles. I pick them up and examine them. The room is buzzing with reddish-orange energy. Ben is hurriedly unpacking the picnic basket onto the floor and rummaging about.

He sneaks up behind me and removes the hair tie that lives around my wrist. He moves slowly and gathers up my long hair, then wraps it with painstaking care, letting wisps of it float down and brush across my cheek. He removes all my clothes except for my matching bra and underwear. I bought those special for him. So I could have a moment like this. He steps back to look at me.

"God, you're beautiful. I want you to be mine forever."

I say nothing. My lips are parted slightly with want. It might be enough just to want him.

He takes my arm and licks from my wrist to the crook of my elbow. Then he picks up a packet of salt and sprinkles it from top to bottom, licking the remnants of salt off the packet before throwing it to the floor. As he cleans the salt from me and throws back his shot, I understand this is about way more than tequila.

"Now you." He brings his wrist to my mouth and I oblige. My mouth is filled with a briny coarseness, and he opens another bottle.

"The whole thing," he instructs.

It burns on the way down and my belly and throat are warm from the amber liquid. Immediately, pleasure blossoms from my chest and I'm relaxed. Weird kind of relaxed. Turned on relaxed.

He tugs on my ponytail. "Do you want another?"

"I want you."

"Let me hear you say it."

"I want you."

"Louder."

"Now!"

He shoves me to the bed and I land in a heap of pillows and blankets, but we don't bother to get under them. He takes off his shirt and straddles me. Then he leans into me, smothering my face with his lips, kissing my forehead, mouth, neck, and back to my mouth again—hungry, never getting enough.

He removes my underwear. I fumble with his belt buckle. I'll never be fast enough. He's in a hurry. He is entering me before even fully removing his pants.

"I want to hear you," he whispers into my ear. "Don't hold anything back. If you feel it, I want to hear it."

A steady bass is vibrating in the background, and the windowpane rattles. He removes himself from me and I arch my back in an instruction to come back in. I want him. I need him.

I can sense him reset the wheels turning and twisting inside his mind. He's going to make me squirm. He kicks off his pants and looks towards the window. He starts at my ear and goes down to my neck. My entire body stills. He cups my breast into his mouth and sucks, first gentle, and then so hard it's almost painful. When I scream out, he presses harder and I'm not sure I can bear it. Then he releases me and moves lower.

His mouth is at my belly and his thumb has moved inside me, teasing. His mouth inches lower. His tongue flickers at the soft inside of my thighs and I'm fighting with myself to let go. The windows are open, the blinds are open, and the lights are on. I can see everything. My vision is blurry, either from the tequila or the heady realization of what's happening to me right now.

He's lower, and then he's there. Soft and smooth at first, then aggressive and angry. His tongue is inside me and it's going deeper than he ever has before. It's as if he *needs* to do this. Determined, hungry, insatiable. Despite trying to keep quiet, a moan escapes, and I flush with embarrassment. But it just makes him go harder. He keeps going and going until my body has

Spectrum

betrayed me and I have come to him. He has me, all of me, and I have no control over it.

My back arches again, this time without my permission, and he digs in. He's going to try and do it again. Every nerve in my body is raw with wicked pleasure. It's so high that I want to cry.

I want to tell him to get off me so that he can come into me with himself and take some of what I'm feeling. It's too much for me. I'll explode from it. It has to stop, but I can't bear for it to end. He's seconds from taking me there again when he flips to his back and positions me on top of his face. I want to back off. This is fifty shades of wrong. I feel like I'll smother him, but he grabs my thighs and pulls me closer. He begs, "Take it. Take me. All of me. Take it now, and I need to hear you."

I grab the top of the head board and start to rock. He moans and everything intensifies. I can't control it now. My body is moving and there's nothing I can do about it. I rock and his tongue thrashes inside me. I'm somewhere else, riding something forbidden. This isn't for girls like me. He has me in his mouth, sucking and licking so deep I get there one last time with a screech and a howl that I'll never know as my own before I collapse beside him, stunned. *What has just happened?*

He scoots up beside me and I whisper, "What about you?"

He only smiles and places his hand on my belly. "This was never about me. Just you, love."

He hops up out of bed, leaving me just a remnant of

whatever I was. He has ruined and rebuilt me all at the same time. Will I ever be the same? Will I turn into some twisted freak that can only get off this way? I'm ashamed of what I've done, but I want to do it again.

He hops in the shower before I have time to be embarrassed in front of him. He's always been the adventurous one in our relationship. I'm not even sure if what we did is called adventurous, but in my world it is. The only other person I've been with is Jude, and we certainly didn't do that.

I lie in bed and look around as the wind whips the flimsy curtains around. I can hear the bustle outside, and the low tones of normal conversations. If I can hear them, then that means—oh God, he did that on purpose. It was an exhibition. Is that part of the thrill? I won't be able to show my face all weekend. Unless I'm someone else.

He opens the shower door thirty seconds later.

"Ready to go check the place out?" He looks cheeky, self-satisfied, impish.

"Yes, but would you like to play a game?"

"I like it. " He bends down and kisses my mouth, and the memory stirs me up again. If we are going to do anything besides fool around this weekend, I'll have to keep that memory at bay. It makes me hungry and irrational.

"So do you have names for us then?" He slides his socks up and removes his perfectly folded jeans from his bag. "How about I pick yours and you pick mine."

"You'll have to tell Sandy. I'm serious. I can't show

my face around here after that freak show of mine if I think anyone will ever walk away with my name. I'm still a little mad about that. A girl's gotta have her virtues." I blush and look down.

"Oh, come on. You still have them. If it makes you feel any better, we've lived out a fantasy of mine."

My face grows hotter and I'm eager to change the subject.

"You're Arthur," I tell him.

"Really, Arthur? Why? Did you have a secret crush on a guy named Arthur? You're killing me here. How can I show *my* face around here if everyone's going to call me Artie?"

"You deserve it."

"Well then, my fair lady. You are Guinevere, but we'll just call you Gwen."

"Are you going to be my Knight?"

"Now, you're getting the story mixed up. If I was going to be your knight, we'd call me Lancelot and we'd have a sordid affair. So what will it be, my fair lady? King or Master of Affairs?"

"Who did she love more?" He takes my foot into his hand and begins to massage as he contemplates his answer. "God, even your feet are soft."

"That's not an answer." I kick at him with toes.

"That depends. She loved Arthur and had a huge amount of respect for him, King and country and everything, but she didn't know any better. Arthur would have been better in the family sense, but then in comes Lancelot and she doesn't really have control over it. It's just something that happens. She's a victim of her own desires. They were destined and doomed."

"Can she have them both?"

"Well, she does for a while, but that can only last for so long."

"Who would you pick? Arthur or Lancelot?" I pull my foot back. Even him touching my feet does things to me.

"Gwen, I choose Gwen." He leans in, moving his hand up my thigh, but I stop him. My knees shake and I scoot away from him. "I need a little time after the last one."

"As you wish, my queen."

It always takes me a bit longer to get ready, and I'm almost relishing it, taking my time on purpose. Things are changing already for us. Is this what we needed all along? The invisible rift neither of us could explain is lifting, and I'm remembering Ben for the man I fell in love with.

He has packed clothes for me perfectly. I unfold my designer jeans that are ripped in all the right places and the black boots that come to just below my knees. I pair them with black tube top that ties at the top and necklaces me in a braided V. Then I assemble my hair in a loose bun with wisps of hair that fall, just the way he likes it. I look in the mirror and study, searching for what he sees in me. It's hard to believe I live my life as an old mom, but in this moment I'm the twenty-five - year old I would have been had I not had Tate so young.

I walk out and see Ben waiting in a chair, watching

me as I exit the tiny bathroom. His knees bounce with nervous energy, like that cat ready to pounce.

"You are stunning." He tosses a mini bottle at me. Jack Daniels.

"I don't think I can drink this. What do you say we head down to the bar? I could use a beer."

I toss it back and he pockets it.

"After you, your highness."

The next few hours are a blur. There's one ridiculously big central tent—Gatsby West Egg big—and it really is a festival more than a wedding. There's a band that switches out every couple of hours, and you'd never be able to guess where the bride and groom were. Word is, nuptials are tomorrow. That's when the real party begins, and it doesn't end until Sunday, when reality will set in and we return to our normal lives.

Ben and I dance until my feet throb. We play a game where we pretend to pick up other people and, when it gets sketchy, we rescue each other. A scene right out of When a Man Loves a Woman, only I'm not an alcoholic and he's not Andy Garcia.

A slow song comes on and he brings me in close. People watch us as if we're the show. I'm sweaty from exertion, and he kisses at my shoulder. The summer heat, vibration of music, and intoxicating smell of Ben is enough to make me never want to leave this moment. I don't care if he proposes or not. I don't care about the problems we have or the problems we don't know we have, but just don't know how to talk about. I just want him. It's him. It's always been him.

"He's here, you know."

"Who's here?" I ask as I back up to see his sweet face. I want to take him in. I've not had much to drink, but I'm drunk on him.

He spins me and gives me a little dip.

"Your boyfriend."

My heart lurches. The idea of anyone I know being here after my spectacle in the cabin earlier makes my stomach churn, and I raise an eyebrow.

"Don't play games." I scowl. "Who's here that I should know about?"

He leans in to whisper in my ear. "Hugo Wiley, lead singer of the River Rats."

"I know. So?"

He spins me again. "He's the one. The one on your list."

And the only one who can sing pink. But I'll never tell him that.

I chuckle. "Should we make a game of it?" I ask as I nuzzle back into his neck.

"Yes."

"You can't be serious." I back up, and he is. "That was just for fun, and you can't want that." I inhale and exhale, feeling the euphoria evaporate.

"I want you to have this. I want you to have everything you've ever wanted. If we make this thing between us forever, I want you to experience everything before you commit to me. Get it out of your system. It's like the fates have aligned. What are the chances that the River Rats would be at the same place at the same time as us, right before we are about ready to hunker down?"

I walk off the dance floor. *Hunker down?* Is that what he thinks this is? What kind of a man wants his girl to chase after some rock star in a band? That can't be love. He's either twisted and not the man I thought he was, or he thinks he's giving me the world. But he must know I won't seal the deal. Either way, he thinks he wins. If he gives me this, he looks like the modern man who can give me everything, be adventurous. What the fuck? If it's the other way, he still wins. Shows me how giving he is, and then I can't pull it off. He thinks I can't pull it off. Then I come back crawling to him and realize he's as good as it gets so I'll never stray again. What the fuck?

"He's married, you know."

"But you'll try?"

"God, what is wrong with you?" I'm actually stomping now as I make my way back to the cabin.

I slam the door in his face, but he quietly opens it and sits down.

"Listen, Sam. I need you to just give me a minute. Hear me out."

I plop down on the bed and the room spins in my misery. Maybe I've had more to drink than I remember, or maybe it's the letdown of realizing the rest of the weekend is gone. I should've known better than to let myself think Ben and I were going to have some kind of rekindling weekend. It's always the same. It's like he gets off on playing with fire.

"Can we say *what if* for the next five minutes? If you hate it, we can be done."

"Okay, let's go. Clock's ticking." I fake look at my wrist, but that's laughable as I've never worn a watch. What I should do is pretend to look at my smartphone. Somehow, I don't see it having the same effect.

"What if I told you it was okay? What if I told you I wanted this too? What if I told you it could make our relationship stronger? What if I told you that if you don't at least try, I'll always wonder? Something's here, Sam. This is too strong a coincidence. You know when I booked this weekend with Sandy, I didn't even know the River Rats were going to be here. You know why? They weren't. They were booked the same day I made the reservation. They were meant to be here, just like you were."

"You want me to sleep with Hugo Wiley?"

He shifts in his seat, but he's holding strong.

"Yes."

"Why?"

"I want you to have that."

"What if I don't want it?"

"Come on. Pretend it's not me you're talking to. Pretend it's one of your girlfriends and you are back home with a bottle of wine and a Hugo Wiley video comes on the television. Where does the conversation go? Have you never once dreamed about what it could be like?"

Is this really happening? Is the boy I fell in love with seducing me to sleep with another man? It's got to be some kind of joke. Some kind of test.

"Hugo Wiley's not even a real person." I lean over and tuck the pillow between my knees. "He's this thing.

Spectrum

Not even real. He's just some guy who sings in a band."

"I know that's not true. Music means something to you. *His* music means something to you. I know you're not into him because you're some kind of groupie wannabe. He speaks to you somehow, more than maybe even me."

"How would you know that?"

"I just do." He looks down and then back up at me. "So are you going to at least try?"

"No. Are you coming to bed or not?"

He stands and makes a move toward the door. He's looking down as he hesitates. "I'm going out for a drink."

I want him to stop. To come back to me. To beg me to come with him. Ask me to go for a drink. Anything. He's leaving me here all by myself, and *he's* angry that I haven't consented to try and sleep with another man. I'm crying for every reason I shouldn't be, and not for the reasons I should be. It's over. It's really over. I'm not sure how we get past this.

I wake up with his arms draped around me and I breathe a sigh of relief. There's a white fog with streaks of black, trapping me in some kind of domestic nightmare. If only it were just a nightmare. The only reason I know it's not is because I'm still wearing what I wore last night. In all the nights I have gone to sleep with Ben, I've never, not once, woken up in anything other than his t-shirt.

He senses I'm awake and scoots in closer.

"I'm really sorry." He sounds stuffed up, so I turn to

look at him.

"Have you been sleeping?" I touch his face and try to remove the devastation.

"No, just waiting for you to wake up."

"Have you been crying?"

"Of course not." He smiles. "Kings don't cry."

"So you are the King now?"

"I want to be. Please give me another chance. I only want what's best for you, what's best for us. Start over?"

"I guess I don't get it." I tousle his hair and he gets up on an elbow to get a better look at me.

"I meant it when I said I want to be with you forever." He traces my chin with his thumb.

"Why does that have to involve Hugo Wiley?"

"Because he's the one. You don't realize it because you're just a baby, but marriage is going to be tough and there are going to be times that you think you didn't live enough, do enough, meet enough people, and at your fingertips is a whole weekend full of rock stars and your childhood crush. Don't you think you'll always wonder?"

"I'm not your ex-wife."

"You are the exact same age she was when we got married."

"I'm not her."

"Maybe you're not. But I'm giving you permission to sow your wild oats. Seriously, I wouldn't say it if I didn't mean it. This time I get married, I want it to be forever. And I want you to look back with no regrets. You've only been with two people. Are you sure this is what you really want?"

Spectrum

"I don't know. Maybe I don't want any of it. Maybe I don't want you or Hugo Wiley. Maybe I'm sick of your games."

I hop out of bed and into the bathroom before he can stop me. I'm in the shower doing nothing but letting the water pelt down on me. The scalding water is making me lightheaded, but I can't come out. Not where he is. Out there. I don't even know who he is.

Part of me wants to make him pay, make him see what he's really proposing. Find Hugo Wiley and throw it in his face. I could never actually go through with it, but what if he thought I did? Would he really think it was such a good idea then?

Music is thumping outside the cabin walls and they shake. I'm getting restless. I've been in here alone all day, feeling sorry for myself while the effects of what sounds like people actually having a good time boom outside. Still no Ben.

With nothing to do, I take another shower, and still no Ben. I do my hair and makeup, and still no Ben. I've put on a pair of daisy dukes and a gray tank top lined with fake diamonds. I spend some more time on my eye make-up. Smoke them up, make me someone else.

I dig through the bag. Here's something I don't own. A slutty black cocktail dress. I put it on and wait for him. Still no Ben. I take it off and go back to the shorts and tank. I fall asleep again.

I wake in a start on the bed, and I'm still alone. I'm really still alone in a love nest built for two. One pathetic girl waiting for a boy. Barely checking the mirror, I give myself one more scan. My hair is trussed from sleeping, eyes still smoked up and, and in shorts looking more punk than mom, I walk out the door.

***

The loudest music is coming from the bar near the lake, so I walk over there. Sandy is bartending, and I breathe a sigh of relief at a familiar face. I'm relieved for more than one reason. Ben has been gone for a really long time.

"Beer please," I say with as much of a smile as I can muster. I refuse to ask her if she's seen him.

Three beers deep and I'm starting to feel better. This must be how alcoholics become alcoholics. Too much of a good feeling without the good sense to know when to stop. I'm not going to stop tonight either. I eye a guy at the end of the bar in a floral Hawaiian shirt sipping something hard, neat.

"Dance?" I ask.

I'm not drunk yet, but somehow I feel a weight being lifted. Tonight will not be about Ben. Tonight will be about me. I'm going to figure out how to be me again, and tonight marks the beginning of the rest of my life.

He eyes me appreciatively, lingering on my legs in the last minute heels I decided to put on. Probably a mismatch on some level, but I feel incredibly sexy, so it's not mixed to me.

I kind of want to push the limits with this guy, but it turns out he *has a daughter my age*, and I am sober enough to take the hint. He keeps an eye on me as I change my dance card from dancer to dancer. I do the two-step, jitterbug, and throw in a few slow dances, always returning to the company of Sandy at the bar.

Spectrum

Then a familiar riff comes from the stage. Only it's not the band, just one guy. Hugo Wiley. He could just be another guy in a band, but there's something special about him. Sure, he looks every bit the rock star, with tattoos that line his forearms and twist with the strums of his guitar, and loose, long hair that hangs in his face, but there's something deeper there. Somewhere in there, there's an artist who speaks in a rainbow. He pushes the hair behind his ear and tests his mic, releasing that voice. Of all the colors in the spectrum, this is my favorite.

I decide in my new buzz for life that I *am* going to be someone else. I go to the front, pretend I'm a tease, and spend the rest of the set making eye contact when he'll let me. Maybe I'm fooling myself, but he gives me an appreciative smile. He announces the last song, and I leave. I'm strong, but not that strong.

Ben was right about one thing, but it's bothering me how he could possibly know. Hugo Wiley has been a part of my life for a long time. When I first heard him, he wasn't part of the River Rats. He was in a group called Funky Monkeys, and he was just getting his start in the world. At the same time my parents were ending theirs in the world of marriage. Hugo would sing to me and drown out their shouting. The louder they got, the more my volume button turned right. Hugo's music, no matter who he plays with, always sounds pink. He went through a rebel phase with shades of orange, but the pink was always there.

Later after the shed of my high school years, I relied on Hugo Wiley to get me through my first heartbreak.

And he was even there for the birth of Tate. Hugo Wiley can't be more than a decade older than me, so why does it feel like he has always existed, like a Redwood that only gets taller year after year?

"How about another one, Sandy?" I go to ask, but she already has one sliding down the bar toward me. A single spray bubbles out as I raise it to my mouth, and I shake my hair out as it sticks to my shoulders.

God, the beer is good. Somewhere in the background, a CD is thrown in and a bass starts pumping through my barstool. Even in this stage of some kind of chemical happiness, I feel someone watching me. I look around, but everyone is the same as me. Stars and common folk mingling together, lost in a world of altered realities and dreams becoming reality.

Blue Baby is still on the dance floor, flying high on something. She's trying to get Hugo Wiley on the floor with her, but he shakes his head and walks over to the bar. She brushes it off and finds her next victim. My Hawaiian shirt father figure follows her to the floor, and I turn back around, becoming oblivious to it all.

"Buy you a drink?" Hugo asks as he scoots into the barstool beside me. I can feel Ben's eyes on me, but he's nowhere to be found.

"I've got one, but I'm not gonna stop you from sitting there." It's kind of blowing my mind that he's actually sitting by me. If this had been even two years ago, I would have died at the sheer luck of this meeting. I don't look at him, but my mind is fixated on his words. Sure, I've seen him interviewed on TV and heard him sing in about every shade of pink there is and even some they don't have a name for, but his voice, just talking, is doing something weird to me. He makes small talk with Sandy, and I sit mesmerized just by his voice.

I turn my attention back to Sandy, but she's busy behind the bar. I'm kind of kicking myself. I've got Hugo Wiley here and I don't know what to say, so I don't say anything. I'm cursing Ben for ruining this for me. Awkward is strung all over me, and I'm sure Hugo can see it.

A bar stool scrapes against the floor and Hugo is close enough to touch. My heart is thundering. Is it the beer, or the fantasy an arm's length away?

"What's your story, girl?" That voice.

I give him a sideways glance and an amused smile.

"I'm going to use the ladies room." I scooch off the stool in one motion, and surprisingly don't trip as I practically bound to the bathroom.

Inside I splash water on my face and straighten up my eye make-up, that's currently more smudged than smoky, and I try not to look like a tramp. I'm ready for this. This is my chance. I can't take too long or he'll get up and leave, and then my chance will be gone forever. Hugo Wiley probably waits for no one.

After a good coaching session, I step outside and finally admit to myself what I've always known. I'm a coward. There's not even a little part of me that's capable of this. Maybe if it weren't for Ben.

Ben's right. Once upon a time, I did make a little deal with myself. If I were ever in my whole life to have a one night stand, it would be Hugo Wiley and only Hugo

Wiley. But back then, there wasn't a Ben to get in the way. Ironically, Ben and I are probably over, but I still can't get myself to the point where I can seal the deal.

Maybe I could. I could just slam a few more beers and remember how Hugo Wiley swaggers when he's in the midst of a song that could seduce me from listening alone, but somehow my mind always works to the after. What then? I'm still Tate's mom. I'm still that girl who doesn't want to give away any part of herself for free, never to get it back.

I don't return to the bar. It's too humiliating. I find myself outside the tent on a picnic table, alone, but somehow watched. I see nothing, but by this point I don't care. There's a bucket of beer at the table, so I crack one and try to figure out what to do with the rest of my life.

When I look up, I see him standing there, just looking at me. How long has he been there?

"Girl, you must got some kind of story," Hugo says as he sits down at the picnic table, straddling the bench, all of his attention on me.

I reach over to the bucket and hand him a beer.

"A girl of a thousand words," he says as he looks wistfully at the stars. "I was going to write a song about that once. I had a dream about it, but when I sat down to write it, it was just gone. I hadn't thought about it until just now. You are her."

I smile and just look at him. I don't feel the need to say anything. No small talk. No niceties. It's probably the surrealism of the moment, or just not wanting to miss a second of whatever this is.

Spectrum

He stands and rubs at his five o'clock shadow not as if it itches, but more as if it were a mannerism he does a hundred times a day. I find myself a little sad I don't know that from experience. I've spent half my life listening to him sing pink and I don't know how he moves in real life.

He looks sharply at me and the blue of his eyes startles me. "So in this dream, I met this girl. Never seen a girl like her before in my whole life. But it wasn't the way she looked, it was the way she carried herself. There was a story and I remember." He paces in front of me, before glancing at me again. "But no matter how many times I asked her, all she did was smile. Seeing you again, or I guess at all, is bringing the whole thing back. Do you believe your dreams tell you the future?"

"Yes. It's actually deja vu. That's where it comes from. Most people haven't figured it out, but that's what it is. I've proven it."

"This I'd love to hear." He sits back down, every bit of him tuned into me, studying.

"Well," I say almost embarrassed, "when I was a kid, I used to write all my dreams down, no matter how small they were. I got really good at it too. Every morning there was a new one. Sometimes they were these epic, strange, fantasy type dreams, but sometimes they were just the normal day to day stuff. One day when I was driving to school, this huge wave of deja vu rolled over me. It was like a tidal wave, really. I turned the car around and went back home. I flipped through that journal until I found it. The exact movements of the day were already documented . . . two years prior.

Hence, deja vu."

"What do you think it means?" He leans in closer and I laugh.

"What'd I say?" He looks genuinely curious.

"Your thousand words are up. I better get going."

"No way, that's not fair. This is just getting good. Don't do me like this. I have one more set. Please just stay for that. We can talk again afterward. Strictly platonic, Scouts Honor." He holds out his hand.

And I take it.

Why not?

If it's fun, why not?

I hate to admit it, but for the next couple of hours I never even think about Ben.

Hugo pulls me onto the stage. When he sees it's a bit too much for me, he pulls another couple of desperately willing girls up with me, and we dance the rest of the set with the likes of the River Rats. Hugo is careful to keep me close to him, and seems to be singing only for me.

Other tents are throwing their own private parties, but I can't imagine there's a better one than here. No amount of alcohol could compete with the intoxication of this night with the River Rats and Hugo Wiley.

Somewhere toward the end of the set, I'm wondering what I'll do. I've set a couple of scenarios in my mind. The later it gets, the less I seem to care and whatever virtues I started with begin to fade. Ben told me to do it. I would be justified. Begged me to even. Does he really believe we'll be stronger after?

Hugo looks over at me again.

I laugh at myself.

It was never a choice.

This thing has been set in motion since I got here. I've had this dream. Deja vu washes over me. He gives me a sideways glance as he croons out the last line of the last song, and reaches for my hand as he thanks the crowd for a good show.

"What now?" I ask, breathless, slutty, wanting.

"Are you sure?" he asks as he pulls me in closer.

"It's set in the stars."

"Says the girl of a thousand words," he shouts out to everyone and no one.

He tosses the half beer that I'd been holding and it sinks into a big rubber garbage, already overflowing with the night's hangover.

My hand in his feels wrong and right. It's almost as if the confusing situation only makes it hotter. It's got some sort of fantasy mixed with revenge. I've never known revenge like this. I feel some kind payback is due. Ben brought me here and did this to me. And then left me. Left me to do this. He deserves everything he gets.

He walks me up the stairs to his tour bus parked behind the main lodge, and I look around. It looks like every bit of what you would imagine a tour bus to look like. I'm nervous for reasons I've never felt before and I'm starting to see a new color.

"Sorry," he mumbles as he picks up random trash and clothes strewn all over the floor. "I wasn't expecting anyone. I don't normally do this, really."

"Oh, shit. You're married, aren't you?" I hover towards the door.

He motions me in. "Sort of. We're separated. Don't let that get in the way. It's just a formality. That's not a line either. She wasn't built for this life." He waves his hand in way a that says he doesn't want to talk about it.

He gets a water bottle out of the mini fridge and hands it to me.

I'm living a moment right out of *Almost Famous*—only the greatest movie of all time—when everything shifts and he picks up his guitar. He's lost in his own world, and somehow I'm there with him. I can hear him talking, but I'm lost somewhere in between.

"Do you mind if I toy with this for a minute?" he asks as he taps on the base of his guitar. Back to here and now.

"Not at all." I smile as this is probably more a part of my fantasy than anything.

He grabs for a pen and a paper and hands it to me as he starts to strum.

"Will you write it down for me?"

He strums the beginnings of something pink, but somewhere in there it turns white and I stop him. This is never going to work if I don't explain it, so I do.

And that's how it went for an hour. He wrote "A Girl of a Thousand Words," and I watched him, writing furiously when he got a line that landed. The pinker the song got, the more excited he got, and I knew he had a hit on his hands.

When he finally finished it, he played it for me and I cried.

Spectrum

"The girl with a thousand words and a thousand tears," he said and, unlike Ben, he didn't try to console me or fix it, or do anything but feel it with me.

"I've been doing this a long time," he finally says, "but it's never felt quite like that. The tears at the end say exactly what I was feeling. How do you do this to me? And the thing with the colors. I have never once heard it described that way, but it's never felt so right. " He laughs. " I've only just met you, but I know you. You're the girl from my dreams. The girl of a thousand words. You're her."

I sit back, exhausted. Something in his words is true; I'm just not sure what.

"I gotta go," I finally say. I try to stand, not wanting to leave, but knowing I have to.

"Can I see you again?"

"What, you mean like tomorrow? I'm with someone. I know, it looks bad. Why am I here?" I inhale deeply, and as I exhale I realize I'm an idiot for everything I'm doing, everything I'm not, and everything I should. "I don't really have a good answer for that, but this is over after tonight."

"Now *that*, I do not accept. You're missing something. That's why you're here. You might think it's the booze or the music or the 'artist' thing, but it's not. There's something about you." He walks over and sits next to me on the undersized couch, then brushes the top of my hand with his thumb.

"Whoever he is, he's an idiot to let you out of his sight. If you were mine, I'd never let you go."

"I'm in love with him," I whisper, and Hugo's eyes

close, maybe to shut me out.

"Close your eyes," he says as he taps along my thigh, and I feel him reach for his guitar. Instinctively, I move just slightly with the music. This should be weird or stiff or awkward, but it's not. He sings "Girl of a Thousand Words" to me one more time, and then asks, "Can I walk you back?"

"I'm good," I say as I stand, and everything in me wishes I could go through with it. It would have been even better than I imagined. Hugo is different. I wasn't some cheap lay. There is something here, and I'm leaving before it even begins.

As I reach the doorway, I turn to look at him. He looks broken, just a boy and his guitar on the couch.

Without looking at me he says, "That's your song. When you hear it on the radio, think of me."

I'm a mixture of relief and sadness when I leave. I can still get out of this. There's still a chance for me and Ben. I've made no irreversible moves. He and Brooke, Tate and I, can still have a life together. I don't care if we get married or not, I just want Ben. I couldn't have given Hugo anything of myself. There was nothing left to give. Ben has it all. I smile at the thought, as I walk back in quick paces to our cabin, 'Forever.'

I open the door and he's a lumpy mess on the bed. My eyes adjust to the dark, and the lump looks too big to be just him.

My stomach is in my throat and it's hard to breathe. Suddenly, I feel sick, like I might actually be sick. I stand over him on his side of the bed. He's lying there in his perfectly handsome package, with a fucking half smile on his face in his sleep. He has on only boxers and a flannel. It's tight in the biceps area, and I imagine the skin below it, tanned, smooth. The shirt is splayed open, haphazardly taken off or a weak attempt to put back on.

I look over to her. It's Blue Baby, with her long dark hair strewn across her face, patches of blue poking out, making it impossible for her to be anyone else. She lies in her drunken stupor on my side of the bed, and in his t-shirt. Of all of it, I think that hurts the most.

His eyes flutter open.

"How does this work?" I ask in a strangely calm voice.

"At about 200 miles per hour," he replies, smiling like a drunk, dumb idiot. It's like he doesn't even see me.

In this moment I realize two things:

He looks beautiful in that stupid, tight flannel shirt, lying there with a ridiculous half smile, lost in some kind of blind oblivion.

I want to scratch his eyes out.

It's the second thing that makes me realize I need to leave. I don't care that I've been drinking. I don't care that I don't know where to go. I don't care that most of me wants to go back to Hugo Wiley. I just need to get out of here.

PART TWO

Hugo

A Girl of a Thousand Words

June

With the memory of the way you looked that night lingering like a sweet hangover, the next morning was a bit of a blur. The only thing I was absolutely certain of was that you were her. You were the Girl of a Thousand Words. You stepped out of my dreams and onto my bus, and something happened that somehow I find easier to describe in colors than words.

You said pink, and it sparked some kind of strange understanding.

"The pinks have shades and you need them to match," you said, and belief began to sweep through like something familiar. Something, I always knew, but had somehow forgotten.

"Remember that song "Show Don't Tell" that you had on your second album?" you asked.

"Of course." The truth of it all trickled out like a dream. It's there, but this idea had to be impossible.

"That one was like watermelon," you said. "The black seeds of chaos mixed in a world where truth is hidden in the flesh of spongy pink, a way to hold it without getting burned. Show, Don't Tell."

"You are bloody brilliant," I said as it finally clicked and I began to strum faster.

You stood then. Your excitement over colors making me fall a little in love with you, at least for the night. "This one you are working on now, Girl of a Thousand Words, think of it as the color of a ballet slipper. It's there. Light, washed with the white of misunderstandings, but put everything you know to be true into it and it will feel like a blush, the pink getting deeper as it gets better. Weird?" You laughed in a way that made me want to bottle it up and keep it to myself forever.

And that's when I knew I had to know you.

Chapter One

Hugo

It's Complicated

August 2014

The song is a terrible hit. Terrible because it belongs to Sam and I can't share it with her. I've gone to her house and stood outside her door too many times to admit without getting arrested. There's this one thing she said that keeps me from knocking. *"I'm in love with him."*

I've considered sending her a copy of *A Girl of a Thousand Words* with my phone number in the off chance she doesn't own a radio, but my better sense keeps me from going through with it. Plus, it feels like kind of a douche move. I've even considered hiring a P.I. to get her whole story, but I'm sticking with my own private stalking for now. It's a little trickier with having to dodge paparazzi, but through watching her outside her doors and good old fashioned Google searches, I've learned a few things about her.

Things I know about Sam:

She has a kid. And a Facebook page dedicated to his father, who died in some kind of accident. She runs the page. In the beginning, she used to write these long beautiful poems to someone who'll never see them. She still maintains the page with new adds here and there, but mostly there's no activity, save for some random picture of old times from friends they must have shared. The oldest I could find, she couldn't have been more than seventeen. Which leads me to fact number two.

The boy's father must have been her high school sweetheart. Is this who she meant when she said "I'm in love with him?" I never considered I'd be competing with a ghost.

She's in a relationship that's "complicated." If it's the ghost she is talking about, it makes for an even more interesting situation. Except there's that guy. He comes and gets the kid about once a week, and the pained look on her face when she opens the door answers my question. He has *complicated* written all over him.

I've got my laptop open, and being on the remembrance page for too long creeps me out, so I seek her out once again.

Samantha Witherspoon, *private*.

What the hell, why not. *Add friend*.

She may not even know it's me. I didn't even have a real Facebook page until I met Sam. Only the fan stuff the label requires us to have. "*Keep in touch with the fans*," they say. They handle that too. So much for keeping in touch with the fans.

This page, I've created just for her. I never thought I'd have the guts to actually reach out to her, but the waiting is killing me.

If she accepts, she will see something out there just for her. Everything true except for the name.

Chapter Two

Hugo

Two Months Earlier

She walks up the stairs on the tour bus, and for just a second my thoughts turn to my wife. Or maybe ex-wife, depending on how quickly she decides to sign the papers.

My thoughts don't stay with her long as I watch this extraordinary girl walk up those stairs. I'd watched her all night, a creature of curiosity, with a kind of softy willowy air that seems to follow her around.

She's nervous in a way that shows she's unsure of her situation. If only she knew she controlled this whole god damn thing. She could ask to bake cookies and I'd be running to the store for flour. I barely know her, but I know she belongs in my life somehow. She's so familiar, I just can't put my finger on it. All I know is that when she's around, the music is more alive for me than it has been for years. She's my own Penny Lane. I hand her a water bottle and she glances to the back wall.

She notices the Almost Famous poster that is curled and frayed, only bits still sticking with leftover Scotch tape.

She giggles and starts to sing Tiny Dancer, and I belt it out with her, feeling myself reach some kind of high just by her presence. This might not be real, and she could just be here as some kind of "Band Aid" but I don't care. I never want this to end.

"It's like we already know each other," she says as she plops down on the couch.

"Weird, isn't it?" I search around for my guitar.

"I didn't see you as the Russell Hammond type." She muses as she looks at the poster.

"What can I say"—I swipe the guitar and fiddle with the strap—"I dig music."

She smiles, and everything about this is right.

"Do you mind if I toy with this for a minute?"

Russell Hammond's finally got a friend. I waited two days, and there she was. It took everything I had not to just lose myself in her profile and study all her pictures, past and present, but I found myself stuck on one thing.

You found me. Those words were written to me, and that's enough for now.

Chapter Three

Hugo

This Thing Called Facebook

Messenger

Her: Russell Hammond, huh?
Me: This Facebook thing is kind of a trip.
Her: What do you mean?
Her: OMG, you only have one friend. Is this your first time? ☺
Me: You're the only reason I'm doing this.
Her: So, Girl of a Thousand Words, pretty big hit.
Me: When Can I See You?! (Me being bold. No wonder everyone likes this internet thing.)
Her: Why now? It's been two months. Hey, what's your profile picture anyway?
Me: I don't know, a walrus I think.
Her: Why? You are so weird.
Me: I don't know. I didn't think it through.
Her: I've got to go. Tate's home.
Me: Wait.
Her:
Me: Are you there?
Her:
Me: Can we talk again soon?
Her:

Me: (This sucks)

She left me to my own devices, so what choice did I have. I've learned some more things about Sam. If she didn't want me to know, she really shouldn't have "added me."

Things I know about Sam continued . . .

She's more beautiful than I remember. Not in the *duck face, check-me-out-I've photoshopped-the-hell-out-of-myself* way, but in the *unassuming-girl-who-doesn't-even-really-like-the-camera-all-that-much* way. The pictures mostly have multiple people in them, but it's as if the lens only finds her.

There's a little boy who looks a lot like her. This must be Tate.

She works as a waitress. I wouldn't have guessed that.

Favorite band: River Rats. Now that I can work with.

Chapter Four

Hugo

The Pursuit

"We have a deal?" I ask the manager of Cherry Bomb, the restaurant/bar Sam works in.

"What's the catch?" he asks. He fits every bit of that stereotype sleazy bar manager, but I don't care for now.

"The catch is that she can't find out." I lay a hundred dollar bill on the counter.

"Whatever you say, man."

"And you're sure she's working?"

"Yeah, yeah, I told you. She's right here on the schedule. You better not be a psychopath. I could get in trouble for this," he says as he puts away some glasses I'm not sure have even been washed. He offers me a beer, but I'm already out the door.

She got the acoustic version of me last time. I'm going to turn it up a notch and really rock this joint. Hopefully make it a place she can't come in without thinking of me. I arrive early the next morning to set up. A couple of the guys even show up to help, probably out of curiosity more than anything. I've got commitments from my drummer and bass player, but couldn't convince my keyboard player, which is fine. I can fill in there. I guess he thought it wasn't any fun to play without pay.

"Who *is* this girl, man? What's gotten into you?" Kyle (bass player) asks as he checks an amp. "Not the greatest stage."

"We have to improvise. They don't even normally have music in here. Owner's giving me a break."

"So, who is she then?" He stops to think about it and then says, "Oh shit, man. She's The Girl of a Thousand Words?"

I don't answer him, but my face is probably the shade of a fucking poinsettia, so I don't really need to. He continues to hassle me, but I just tune him out. I check everything, and then check it again. And then maybe check it again. It has to be perfect. We leave just in time, as I see a white Honda pull in and the Girl of a Thousand Words exiting her car while tying a black apron on. I want to watch her for a little while, but I'm trying to keep the creep factor down.

I haven't been able to concentrate all day. She has an eight-hour double and should close the place down. We're set to show up around six, sneak in, and start playing without her even knowing what's happening until she hears us. That's the plan, anyway.

Kyle's having about as much fun with this as I am. He's always enjoyed a good ruse. Missy (drums) makes sure I know this is only a favor to me and "we're too big for this," but I can't complain since she actually showed up.

I call the owner, and he sends Sam to the back to stock some freezer shelves. I don't even have time to look around and take the place in. Owner must have talked to someone, because it feels packed. Like

Saturday-night-at-the-arena packed. There's not a place to sit anywhere, and I doubt they're here for the food.

Everything's set, and Kyle rips out the first chord. It silences the room, and all eyes are on us. We're starting with "Show, Don't Tell," and it's obvious everyone in here knows who we are, as cheers erupt. This is going better than I imagined. Now I just need to see her.

But it's not her I see. It's the guy from all the Facebook pictures. The guy who picks up Tate once in a while. He's sitting at the bar, and he looks as stunned as me. It's like we know each other, but we don't. He looks from his drink, back to me. He's wondering what I'm doing here. I'm wondering the same thing.

Then I see her. She has an amused smile on her face. She's carrying a tray of glasses, and she doesn't miss a beat. I nod at her, and she nods back appreciatively as she slides the glasses onto the bar and hits the crowd. It's almost too bad the place is packed. I kind of hoped she'd be able to enjoy the show, but it looks like tonight she's going to get worked.

The joy of the music is back, and I think it's because of her. It's like a private show for her, but she's doing her thing and I'm doing mine. I'm trying to avoid the guy at the bar who sits in that chair as if it's his, and I try not to let it bother me.

The first set is over and I catch a glance of her. Sam and the guy are arguing—not that you could hear it over all the noise—and I find myself wishing he would just go away. It's mostly her yelling, and I'm torn by it. I like that she's giving him hell, but it might be better if she didn't give a damn. He grabs his coat and he's out the door. Just in time.

I let the crowd know that we're on break, but the drunks stay on the floor and sway to the canned music blaring top-40 hits.

I try to talk to her a couple of times, but she just smiles at me and mouths "*I'm sorry*," as she carts more beers to more guys who don't need them. I smile as I consider her tips will probably be good tonight.

I'm getting nowhere, so I decide to obey my ADD and find something to do. I slide behind the counter, and the owner moves to the side. He knows what I'm thinking. It's the only chance I get to see Sam as she comes back for refills. My younger days are coming back to me when I had to bartend to pay the bills. There's another bartender with obvious experience, and we take to each other right away. I soon find myself bartending "Cocktail" style.

He tosses a bottle of gin into the air. I catch it, then empty the contents into a glass of ice and slide it down the counter. He laughs like he knows he's getting laid tonight and tosses another. I fill the martini shaker and throw it back to him behind my back. He catches it in perfect sync, shakes it, and fills his own glass.

"You looking for a job?" he asks as he gets back to a gaggle of ladies swooning over him, some sneaking smokes, enjoying the last of their youth.

I'm having such a good time, I almost forget Sam's out slaving away. Maybe watching her in her element is part of the good time.

"Is there anything you can't do?" she yells over the music and holds up four fingers. "Bud Light."

I use the side of the counter to pop the lids off for her, and place them on a tray. She leaves the tray and weaves the tops between her fingers, and she's gone before I can even answer.

The line is never-ending, and I could stay behind the bar all night. But the break is up and I'm back on stage. I smell like an ashtray, but I don't care.

"Okay, okay," I say to the crowd, absolutely alive with booze and music.

"We're going to slow this down a bit. This one's called *A Girl of a Thousand Words,* and it's dedicated to someone who looks better in a pair of jeans than a dress, and I mean that in the best way." I wink down at a fan in the crowd, and she obviously thinks this is about her.

I look back up at Sam, and she smiles at me. I'd do this every night for the rest of my life if that's what it took to keep feeling the way I do right now.

Show's over, and Sam is nowhere to be found. It'd be my luck to end on this note. I'd allowed myself to think this was our turning point, and maybe I'd have a chance with her, but she's just gone. I look up to the owner, and he points his thumb as if *she's out back.*

I open the door to the back. She must be behind the commercial garbage cans, because I can hear her but not see her, and she's not alone. I can only imagine who it is.

"It's over, Ben. The sooner you get that, the better off you'll be. If you keep getting drunk like this, I'm not going to let you see Tate anymore. You need to get a grip."

I shouldn't, but I walk in a little closer. It could be the only way I can get the truth from this mysterious girl.

"Don't do that. It wouldn't be good for either one of us."

"You leave him out of this! I'll decide what's good for him."

"I'm sorry. I know. Please, this is just coming out so wrong. Are you sure you didn't know he was going to be here?"

"God, no. I haven't seen him since that night. But what does it matter? You have no say in my life anymore."

"I know, I know. I just don't want to see you get hurt."

"Too late."

I slip inside before she catches me. Besides, it was starting to feel too personal. I'm not sure what I was thinking with this girl.

Two more things I've learned about Sam:

She's in love with a dead guy.

She's also in love with someone who obviously doesn't deserve her.

And one thing about me:

I'm losing my mind.

Thankfully, the band has everything packed up and I can't get out fast enough. The owner tries to stop me, something about coming back again, but I can't take this anymore. This is just me making another bad decision.

When I get home, there's a message waiting for Russell Hammond.

Sam: Where'd you go?

Me: Where've you been?
Sam: What's that supposed to mean?
Me: I'm not sure there's room in your life for me.
Sam:
Me: Tell me I'm wrong.
Sam: I'm not sure that I can.

Two weeks go by and I haven't heard from Sam. I've written a dozen songs, but they're all garbage. I've tried to hear the colors like she does, but without her it's just a blank canvas.

I look around my hotel room and fight the urge to destroy it all. I don't drink much, so that's out. I don't do drugs, so that's out. (Some rock star I am.) I don't have a girlfriend to talk me through whatever this is, and the music is already written, it just doesn't speak to me. I glance at the computer and fight every fucking urge I have to look at her profile. I get in the car and drive. Girl of a Thousand Words comes on the radio. I turn the station and the messenger on my iPhone pings.

Sam: You there?
Me: Always (Lame. Did I just write that? How can I delete it?)
Sam: Are you for real? (Too late to delete.)
Me:
Sam: Can I see you?
Me: Everything in me wants to say yes.
Sam: Then do it.
Me: I don't want to be number four.
Sam: What is that supposed to mean?
Me: This is going to sound embarrassing, but I know

Spectrum

a lot about you.

Sam: Enlighten me.

Me: I guess, the way I see it, I'll be number four. Tate I would imagine is number one, the ghost of his dad number two, Paul Bunyan number three, and me number four. I haven't even considered possible parents and friends who might beat me out too. The highest I could ever climb in your life would be number four.

Sam: This is a pretty deep conversation to be having on messenger. Paul Bunyan, huh?

Me: That guy's huge. Boyfriend?

Sam: Ex. Paul Bunyan, that's funny. He's even got his Babe the Blue ox.

Me: What does that mean?

Sam: Long story.

Me: I've got time.

Sam: Remember that wedding we met at?

Me: How could I forget?

Sam: He cheated on me with Blue Baby that night.

Me: Shit, that's heavy. Why do I feel like this is shifting into the friend zone? Maybe we should talk about something else.

Sam: God, yes.

Me:

Sam: That was really cool what you did.

Me: Help me out here. I'm new to this messenger thing. I can't see or feel your emotion. Is that sarcasm? (Have I mentioned voice text is amazing? Call me a sucker for the little microphone.)

Sam: Emoticons help?

Me: What's an emoticon?

Sam: Never mind. I mean what you did at my work. I don't think I've ever had that much fun before.

Me: It was pretty great.

Sam: How many other tricks you got up your sleeve?

Me: (Fumbles with hand texting now. How weird would it be if she heard me?) Open your door.

"Hey," her beautiful mouth says when she opens the door. "You *are* full of tricks."

"Is this a good time?" I ask as I shift the guitar strap on my shoulder.

"It's perfect. Tate's in bed. You go everywhere with that?" she asks, pointing at the guitar.

"I need your help, Muse."

She opens the door to let me in, and I see a little boy standing in the hallway. He's what she may have looked like as a child. He has the same thick yet wispy dark hair and intelligent blue eyes.

"You must be Tate," I say and hold out my hand. And he actually walks over to me to shake it.

"Tate," Sam says disapprovingly. "You're supposed to be in bed."

"I'm calling Ben."

"Oh, no you're not. I'm the mother and you're not in charge here."

"He's nervous. Maybe he shouldn't be here." The boy says. I notice he's wearing footie pajamas. God, I haven't seen those in years.

"Who's nervous?" Sam asks, cocking her head in curiosity.

"He is," Tate says, pointing at me.

"How do you know that?" she asks as she leans down

to him.

He turns his back to me, but I can still hear him. "Because it's the same as when I went to school. It feels the same."

"What do you mean it feels the same?" she asks.

"I'm not lying!" he cries and runs into his room.

"Oh shit," Sam says, but I already realize I've been here about five minutes longer than I should have.

"This is me. This is the kind of stuff I deal with. You sure you're up for it?" she asks as she glances toward Tate's room.

I question her with only a look.

"Well, I've suspected it for about a year now. He has what I have; only it's different. When I first found out about synesthesia—you know, the hearing colors thing? They told me it was hereditary. I just assumed he would have mine if he got anything at all."

"I'm not following."

"I guess I can't be sure, but there's another one called mirror synesthesia. It's rare, but if you have it, you literally feel the same sensation that another person feels. He's always been a quiet, sensitive kid. You know last week I was cooking and I burned my hand, and he actually withdrew his hand and screamed at the exact time I burned myself?"

"He must still be pretty tight with Paul Bunyan?"

"He's like a father to him." She plays with a hem of her ridiculously short shorts that really seem unfair in this particular moment.

I readjust the strap that's pinching at my shoulder. "This was a bad idea tonight. I think I'm just gonna go."

"I can't just pull Ben out of his life, he's been there too long. I have to think about Tate." She exhales so loudly, I'm sure the kid hears.

I'd like to reach out and touch her arm, but somehow it feels wrong. I hook my thumbs to the inside of my pockets instead. I read somewhere that it exudes confidence. I lean against the wall, more confidence. "I'm not asking you to. This is just more complicated than I anticipated. I just need to think about it."

She looks towards her son's door before looking back to me. "Fair enough. How about tomorrow I come over and we work on that music? I could use a distraction." She smiles, finally.

"Deal."

PART THREE

Ben

I'm Only Human

You've been gone three months now. Not really gone, but gone in all the ways I yearn for. I'm grateful you still let me see Tate. I keep imagining that it has an expiration date, once you realize that I'm no good for him and once you find out who I really am. It will come on all of a sudden. I will show up at the door for him and it won't open. I'll knock and knock and it just won't open.

The worst of it is the way you look at me. I took that for granted before. How did I not see the light in your eyes when every morning we would wake up to our Great Perhaps? Now all I see is pain. Different pain. I've known pain in your eyes before, and did everything I could to take it away. I blew it and I still can't even tell you why. Sounds like a half-ass excuse, even in my own mind, but it breaks me when I see I've put that look back into your eyes.

I keep going back to that night. It plays over and over again in my head. Big chunks are missing, and big chunks are burned so deep, I'm afraid they'll never go away. When I reached out to feel you in the warmth of my shirt, only to see it wasn't you, all I could think of was your heartbreak and how you would surely throw me away. And you should.

And now there's him. Who knew Hugo Wiley would actually become a part of your life. How could I possibly compete with that? Truth? I can't. And maybe I shouldn't. Maybe I should let you go. I've seen how happy he makes you. Happier than I ever could. With him, you could have a fresh start. Maybe a chance to forget liars and cheaters, and people who die on you, but, I can let you go. I can do that for you.

Chapter One

Ben

Losing It

"So you'll have him back tomorrow afternoon?" Sam asks as she hands me his bag.

"Can you wait in the truck, Buddy?" I ask Tate. He takes his bag from me and walks slowly down the hallway.

He's gauging us. It's not fair, really. He doesn't even have to ask. He's checking to see how we feel. I'm not sure how he does it. Whether he looks for facial clues, or if it's just some kind of intuition.

"We need to talk about that," Sam says as he turns the corner.

"So he finally told you?"

A flash of hurt crosses her face. "It's really not fair that he trusts you more."

"It's not that. I just get him."

"And I don't? Whatever, that's not the point. That's actually where I'm going. I'm going to see a doctor. I've been talking on the phone with him. They said he might need a special tutor. Homeschooling might be good for him."

"Why aren't you bringing him?"

"I don't want him to feel like a freak."

"Then don't homeschool."

"Since when are you the expert?" She folds her arms across her chest and tries to look at anything but me.

"Don't you want him to feel like he's every other kid?"

"But he's not."

"He doesn't need to know that." I hesitate, ready to leave, but if I don't do something about this, it's going to eat me alive. I don't know why I've held it in so long. Could our story have been different if I had just told her?

"Sam, there's something else. There's something else I need to say. Can we get together when you get back?"

"I don't have time for games. Just tell me now." She's thinking about closing the door. I've pissed her off, but I really don't know how else to do this. She plays with her hair, something she only does when she is feeling "orange."

"I'll talk to you when I get back. I'm going into The Cities tonight. We have the appointment in the morning and then I'll be back after that."

"We."

"None of your business."

"Shit, Sam. Don't mean it still don't hurt."

I walk away before I get myself too worked up. As much as I think Tate's new skill is pretty freaking awesome, I don't need him reading it off me, especially when it has to do with his mother.

It's finally time, I guess. I think it's time that I accept there are no possible ways to have secrets anymore. Not with the way Tate is now. It will hang on between the two of us. It's finally time I take this head on. In some ways, I think my secrets had a way keeping Sam at arm's length. We were always hiding the truth. She couldn't talk about him and I couldn't talk about *them*.

I pull into Tate's grandparents' driveway and put the truck into park.

"You're nervous," he says matter-of-fact-like.

"You could say that," I say back. Maybe a five-year-old shouldn't be my best friend, and maybe I shouldn't be relying on his advice to put me in this position right now. I can't help but think of how furious Sam would be if she knew.

"It'll be fine. They're really nice people," he says as he crooks his head to me. His front tooth looks a little more wobbly today. Sam will be livid if his first tooth falls out when he's with me.

"I don't know how to do this, Tator Tot. Do I just tell them? Are you going to be there? No, that's probably a bad idea. Can you wait in your room while I talk to them?"

"This is your family, Ben. You're my family," he says as he runs his tongue over that wiggly tooth. He outstretches his hand and places it at my chest. It's like he knows exactly what to do. God, I don't deserve him.

He hops out of the truck and is already halfway up the walkway before I can stop him.

"Tate, I'm not sure I can do this. This might be a bad idea."

The front door opens. It's her. His grandmother. My mother. I don't have to do this. The only people who know are me and the little guy, and I wouldn't even have to tell him I'd changed my mind. He'd know. I wonder if that has a color.

She looks at me for the first time. I've never done anything more than wait in the car for the last two years. Sure, I've driven by here so many times they probably have me on neighborhood watch, but I've never actually gotten this close.

"Tate?" she calls to him. "What's going on?" She looks back up to me.

"We need to talk," I say to her, my voice shaky. And then he shows up at the door. Tate's grandfather, and my father. Or at least that's what it says on my birth certificate.

Tate disappears through the doorway, and they invite me in.

"You must be Ben," the man says, and extends his hand. "We've heard a lot about you." He spends just a second studying my face and it feels like he knows.

When I walk in, I'm hit with a flood of so many emotions; I don't even know how to dissect them. I've been over this a hundred times in my mind. My plan to do this devoid of feelings is folding right before my eyes.

All I can see when I look at them are a couple of frauds. They look the piece of perfect parents. They have everything. Perfect ranch style home, double garage, and fuck I think there are even cookies baking in the oven. I see on their wall in the kitchen that they have about a half dozen pictures of Jude, but not a single one of me. He's not even here, but he lives in this house more than I ever would.

Time to just get it over with.

Spectrum

"Mr. and Mrs. Van Erem, I think I'm your son."

She drops her cup of coffee.

"Son, I mean Ben, you must be mistaken," the man says. It's irritating, but I think I may have his nose.

"Just tell me the truth. I don't want anything from you. Did you have a son born on August 28, 1981, in Sioux Falls, South Dakota?"

"Oh, God, James, it's him. He looks like Jude." She flutters around the kitchen, and I realize this is definitely not how I saw this going down. I actually feel kind of sorry for her.

"Why didn't you tell us sooner?" he asks. "You've been around for two years. You could have come to us."

"It had nothing to do with you. It's because of Sam. I'm in love with her. I have been since the moment I first saw her. Shit, I even quit school trying to avoid her. When I found out who you were, it led me to Tate and then her. If she'd known who I was, she never would have been able to get over it. She'd have never seen me for me. I wanted to tell her. I just couldn't."

He only nods, and she is crying.

The rest of it is a bit hazy. I expected them to tell me some kind of crazy story about child abduction, or maybe a different father, a woman who'd been raped, but that's not what I get.

"Ben, we were so young," he says. His head hangs low and I can sense he wants to comfort his wife, but for now he's focused on me.

"But you're still together?"

"I guess so."

"And what about Jude? He's only five years younger

than me? Why keep him?" I ask her. I want to hear her say it.

Her voice is shaky, but she seems determined. "Back then, with you, we thought we were going our separate ways. James was going to college and I was going to take over my family's business. Times were different back then," the woman says. "It wouldn't have been fair to you."

"Fair? Do you know where I wound up?"

Fear flashes across her face and she reaches out to touch my hand.

I snatch it away. "The Muellers. Perfect on paper, I guess. Humanitarians. Is that why you chose them?"

"We didn't know their names. Just that they tried for a child for years. We thought they would give you everything we couldn't."

"Well, my real mother was a nanny for about sixteen years, until the Muellers were killed as missionaries in Sudan. The Muellers never really wanted a kid, they just thought that was what humanitarians did. Adopt needy children. They dumped me with the nanny as soon as they figured out traveling with a kid wasn't all that fun. You know you would think seeing the two of you together would be comforting, but it's not. It just makes me wonder why you couldn't keep me."

I get up. I really feel done here. I call Tate down.

"You're taking him?" She looks almost frantic.

"I better not. I'm not feeling well. Might not be safe to drive with him."

Tate walks down and my chest heaves in a sob as I hug him goodbye.

I look up to them one more time. "Don't tell Sam. It

Spectrum

needs to be me."

PART FOUR

Sam

The Great Perhaps

I nuzzle into Tate's neck as the morning light peeks in through the curtain cracks, and the alarm signals it's time to get up for another day. The radio DJ proclaims it's going to be a beautiful fall morning. "Time to get outside. Seize the day," he says, and it makes me think of you.

"Good morning, Tator Tot," I whisper to the boy who continues to be the reason I get up, when all I really want to do is throw the covers over and never see the outside world again. He also makes me think of you.

He squeezes his little arms around my neck and I just hold him. This is getting easier, but I'm lying to myself when I don't admit that it hurts every damn day.

The beginning was worse. You begging at the door during the day, knocking, refusing to leave, and sobbing outside my window at night. You told me once kings don't cry.

I was out of my mind. I didn't realize. I saw the two of you. I thought you were with him. I don't know what was wrong with me. It just hurt so bad. And there she was. I don't know why. It just happened. It happened so fast. I saw you with him and I just assumed. I was an idiot. I thought you needed to get it out of your system. I'm such an idiot. I see it now. Please, Sam. Just please, you said.

It took me a while to realize that I played a part in all this too. It was my idea to have a list in the first place. What if I had never brought it up? What if we'd never had that conversation? How could a joke get so twisted?

You just wouldn't go away, and part of me didn't want you to, but some part of me did. I finally had to call the cops. Sorry about that, but you can only keep the radio blasting for so long.

Finally, I packed your stuff. The hardest to pack were your t-shirts, soft with the memory of you, hard with the memory of her.

I lie in bed and wonder where you are. The radio switches back to music and "Girl of a Thousand Words" plays, so I sneak over and turn it down. Just another reminder of the night that changed my life, changed our future. Tate sneaks over and turns it back up.

I lie flat on my back, stare at the ceiling, and let myself feel it. Hugo was some kind of dream, you some kind of nightmare, but what kind of fool am I to know I ache for the nightmare?

"Are you sad, Mommy?" Tate asks as he brushes the tears away.

"Yes, and it's okay to be sad, baby. All feelings are okay, we just need to feel them. Let them be what they need to be. Feel the bad ones long enough and they don't feel so bad anymore. Feel the good ones and remember they will come again." Why didn't we know this back then? It could have saved us.

But he's not listening. He's already scampered off. I watch the beauty walk through my doorway and smile at his future.

The doctor says he has an interesting future, to the say the least. His childhood will be the hardest when he has to figure out how to control feeling other people's emotions and block them out when he needs to. For now, we're working this thing out together.

This little five-year-old boy knows more than he ever should. It took two meetings with Hugo for Tate to figure out Hugo was only using me for my ability to hear colors and piece the music together just by blending them. Hugo might not even have known what he was up to, might have even been confused by it himself, but Tate said it all when he told me that when Hugo looks at me "all he sees is music."

Tate's words proved even truer when I told Hugo and he only responded with a short letter of thanks, some flowers, and news he was hitting the road again.

There's one good thing that came out of all this. Tate finally trusts me. The wall that was between us for so long was the pain I felt about Jude. Tate could feel that too. It was too much for him to bear. Can you imagine what I put him through? A child having to mourn for a man he never knew. I'm learning to let that go too. He tells me all we get is today. Can you picture that? He must have read it on a poster at the doctor's office. I don't know. Maybe he got it from you.

This will be the last letter I send you. Please find a way to forget about The Great Perhaps.

A New Chapter

Sam

Talk or Fix

My cell phone buzzes in my purse on the floor, but I leave it. It's Saturday and it can wait. It buzzes again. I dig through until I find it. It's set to *low*, and I see I've missed fourteen calls from an unknown number.

Sandy. Fourteen missed calls from Sandy. Car accident. Hospital.

I can't do this again.

Dropping Tate off at the neighbor's is a blur. Walking through the hospital doors is a blur. How could this be happening again? Everything is flooding back. Accident. Jaws of life. Time of death.

They don't even tell me which room Ben's in. I know. It's like I'm drawn to him and he's pulling me where I need to go. It feels like deja vu, but it's not because it was a dream. It's because it's happened before. But I must be dreaming because Tate's grandparents are here too.

I drop to my knees and I'm there. Three years ago, and it's happening again, right now.

"Don't let her in here!" the doctor yells. "She's in shock, keep her out!"

I don't listen, I follow him in. How is it he's in pieces and I'm standing here, not a scratch on me? I was just with him. He was just smiling at me, teasing, celebrating our future. Our future with a baby. Screeching tires and a boom so loud it didn't sound real. Some kind of truck. Then the world went black, gray, and now the stark white of the hospital walls. I refuse to leave, and they soon forget I'm in the room. There's blood everywhere. Every part of him is mangled. His face is purplish blue and swollen, arms bent and limp, heart not beating. They continue to work feverishly when I hear the worst words I will hear for as long as I live.

"Call it. Time of death."

He left me. He broke all of his forever promises. He's gone. Promises gone. Left Tate too, and didn't even bother to meet him first. And now Ben's leaving. As I sit crumpled on the floor outside his room, I beg. Please, not again. I don't care what he's done. Please, just not him. God, I can't do this again. It's why I am the way I am. It's why no one gets in. There's too much pain. I'll change, I swear. Just not him.

Sandy comes out of his door and she's smiling. Everything about this moment feels blackishly wrong.

"He's asking for you," she says, and I crumple. *Asking for me? Alive, breathing, asking for me?*

I walk in dazed, but the instant I see him Indigo explodes in the room, and I don't care what he's done. We might not have a shot at a real relationship again, but I need him in my life. I need him in our life.

I don't say anything at first because the look on his face is enough to shut me up for the rest of my life. The humbled King. Somewhere in that infuriatingly beautiful face is pain, hurt, remorse, and hope.

"You're okay."

He smiles and the blue of him is almost too much. "Talk or fix?"

"Talk."

"I was hoping you'd say that."

The End

Kay Kadinger

Spectrum

Color Key

Blue – love, when something's right
Red – deception or something wrong
Orange – rebellion
White – when something's unknown
Black – chaos
Pink – Hugo's music
Yellow – curious
Rust colored – how things work

Music

Usually there are multiple albums that I listen to while writing. If I could sum up this story with four songs they would be Stay by 30 Seconds to Mars, Dark Paradise by Lana Del Rey, Fade Into You by Mazzy Star, and Human by Christina Perri. I think I wrote the whole story with these songs on repeat.

To the Reader

Spectrum is a self-published novella. In the world of Indie publishing, the most valuable thing to the author is her reviews. If you enjoyed Spectrum and even if you didn't, I'd love to hear from you. A new review is like opening presents on a frost filled Christmas morning. You can find a place to put your opinions of Spectrum on Goodreads and Amazon.

Acknowledgements

Amy, I'm not even sure there are enough thanks in the world for showing me the ropes and helping shape this thing called Spectrum.

March, who will always be Meg to me, thanks for all of your help. I hope to be as good as you someday.

Terry, thanks for encouraging me with my voice and all the help with the story and blurb. Thanks for always being so nice to me. I see we're still friends on Facebook despite my annoying tendencies. Someday we'll have pie.

My betas, the two Jens, Cheer, and Casey, I was treading uncharted waters and your encouragement made this so much fun. Shirley, seriously, you are the bomb. Mysti, my last minute proofer, you're a lifesaver.

Credits
Cover design by Amy Queau
Editing by Jennifer Sell

Made in the USA
Charleston, SC
04 September 2015